The Cuckoo Bird

Written by Carol Krueger

Rigby

Look at this bird.
It is a cuckoo bird.
It will **not** make a nest.
It will **find** a nest with
eggs in it.

3

Look at this bird.
It makes a nest for its eggs.
When this bird goes away,
the cuckoo will come.

reed warbler

reed warbler eggs

The cuckoo bird comes and
takes out one egg.
Then it lays its egg
in the nest and goes away.
It will not come back.

cuckoo egg

reed warbler eggs

The baby cuckoo comes
out of the egg.
It will push all the eggs
out of the nest.
It will push all the baby birds
out, too.

baby cuckoo

baby bird

baby cuckoo

The mother bird
comes back to her nest.
She gets food for
the baby cuckoo.
But the baby cuckoo
is not her baby.

baby cuckoo

The baby cuckoo gets bigger and bigger. It can fall out of the nest, but the mother bird will still get food for it.

nest

The mother is small.
The baby cuckoo is very big!

Cuckoo Bird Life Cycle

The cuckoo finds a nest and lays an egg in it.

The baby cuckoo comes out of the egg. It pushes the eggs out of the nest.

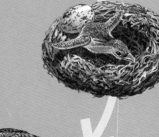

The cuckoo gets big and flies away.

The baby cuckoo gets food from a mother bird.

Index

Guide Notes

Title: The Cuckoo Bird

Stage: Early (3) – Blue

Genre: Nonfiction

Approach: Guided Reading

Processes: Thinking Critically, Exploring Language, Processing Information

Written and Visual Focus: Photographs (static images), Index, Labels, Caption, Life Cycle Diagram

Word Count: 143

THINKING CRITICALLY
(sample questions)

- Look at the front cover and the title. Ask the children what they know about cuckoo birds.
- Read the title to the children.
- Focus the children's attention on the index. Ask: "What are you going to find out about in this book?"
- If you want to find out about a cuckoo laying eggs, which page would you look on?
- If you want to find out about baby cuckoos, which pages would you look on?
- Look at pages 6 and 7. Why do you think the cuckoo bird takes one egg out of the nest?
- Look at pages 12 and 13. Why do you think the mother keeps feeding the cuckoo after it has fallen out of the nest?

EXPLORING LANGUAGE

Terminology
Title, cover, photographs, author, photographers

Vocabulary
Interest words: cuckoo, nest
High-frequency words: then, takes
Positional words: in, out

Print Conventions
Capital letter for sentence beginnings, periods, commas